Alfred Tennyson

The Holy Grail

With drawings by W.L. Taylor

Alfred Tennyson

The Holy Grail
With drawings by W.L. Taylor

ISBN/EAN: 9783337284541

Printed in Europe, USA, Canada, Australia, Japan

Cover: Foto ©Andreas Hilbeck / pixelio.de

More available books at **www.hansebooks.com**

THE HOLY GRAIL·

The Holy Grail

By Alfred Lord Tennyson

With Drawings by

W. L. Taylor

D. Lothrop Company Publishers

Boston MDCCLXXXVII

THE HOLY GRAIL

THE HOLY GRAIL

FROM noiseful arms, and acts of prowess done
In tournament or tilt, Sir Percivale,
Whom Arthur and his knighthood called The Pure,
Had pass'd into the silent life of prayer,
Praise, fast, and arms; and leaving for the cowl
The helmet in an abbey far away
From Camelot, there, and not long after, died.

And one, a fellow-monk among the rest,
Ambrosius, loved him much beyond the rest,
And honor'd him, and wrought into his heart
A way by love that waken'd love within,
To answer that which came: and as they sat
Beneath a world-old yew-tree, darkening half
The cloisters, on a gustful April morn
That puff'd the swaying branches into smoke
Above them, ere the summer when he died,
The monk Ambrosius question'd Percivale.

"O brother, I have seen this yew-tree smoke,
Spring after spring, for half a hundred years:
For never have I known the world without,
Nor ever stray'd beyond the pale: but thee,
When first thou camest — such a courtesy
Spake thro' the limbs and in the voice — I knew
For one of those who eat in Arthur's hall;
For good ye are and bad, and like to coins,
Some true, some light, but every one of you
Stamp'd with the image of the King: and now
Tell me, what drove thee from the Table Round,
My brother? was it earthly passion crost?"

" Nay," said the knight; "for no such passion mine.
But the sweet vision of the Holy Grail
Drove me from all vainglories, rivalries,
And earthly heats that spring and sparkle out
Among us in the jousts, while women watch
Who wins, who falls; and waste the spiritual strength
Within us, better offer'd up to Heaven."

To whom the monk: "The Holy Grail!—I trust
We are green in Heaven's eyes; but here too much
We molder—as to things without I mean—
Yet one of your own knights, a guest of ours,
Told us of this in our refectory,
But spake with such a sadness and so low
We heard not half of what he said. What is it?
The phantom of a cup that comes and goes?"

"Nay, monk! what phantom?" answer'd Percivale,
"The cup, the cup itself, from which our Lord
Drank at the last sad supper with his own.
This, from the blessed land of Aromat—
After the day of darkness, when the dead
Went wandering o'er Moriah—the good saint,
Arimathæan Joseph, journeying brought
To Glastonbury, where the winter thorn
Blossoms at Christmas, mindful of our Lord.
And there awhile it bode; and if a man
Could touch or see it, he was heal'd at once,
By faith, of all his ills. But then the times
Grew to such evil that the holy cup
Was caught away to Heaven, and disappear'd."

To whom the monk: "From our old books I know
That Joseph came of old to Glastonbury,
And there the heathen Prince, Arviragus,
Gave him an isle of marsh whereon to build;
And there he built with wattles from the marsh
A little lonely church in days of yore,
For so they say, these books of ours, but seem
Mute of this miracle, far as I have read.
But who first saw the holy thing today?"

"A woman," answer'd Percivale, "a nun,
And one no further off in blood from me
Than sister; and if ever holy maid
With knees of adoration wore the stone,
A holy maid; tho' never maiden glow'd,
But that was in her earlier maidenhood,
With such a fervent flame of human love,
Which being rudely blunted, glanced and shot
Only to holy things: to prayer and praise
She gave herself, to fast and alms. And yet,
Nun as she was, the scandal of the Court,
Sin against Arthur and the Table Round,
And the strange sound of an adulterous race,
Across the iron grating of her cell
Beat, and she pray'd and fasted all the more.

"And he to whom she told her sins, or what
Her all but utter whiteness held for sin,
A man well nigh a hundred winters old,
Spake often with her of the Holy Grail,
A legend handed down thro' five or six,
And each of these a hundred winters old,
From our Lord's time. And when King Arthur made
His Table Round, and all men's hearts became
Clean for a season, surely he had thought
That now the Holy Grail would come again;
But sin broke out. Ah, Christ, that it would come,
And heal the world of all their wickedness!
'O Father!' asked the maiden, 'might it come
To me by prayer and fasting?' 'Nay,' said he,
'I know not, for thy heart is pure as snow.'
And so she pray'd and fasted, till the sun
Shone, and the wind blew, thro' her, and I thought
She might have risen and floated when I saw her.

"For on a day she sent to speak with me,
And when she came to speak, behold her eyes
Beyond my knowing of them, beautiful,
Beyond all knowing of them, wonderful,
Beautiful in the light of holiness.
And 'O my brother, Percivale,' she said,
'Sweet brother, I have seen the Holy Grail:
For, waked at dead of night, I heard a sound
As of a silver horn from o'er the hills
Blown, and I thought, "It is not Arthur's use
To hunt by moonlight"; and the slender sound
As from a distance beyond distance grew
Coming upon me — O never harp nor horn,
Nor aught we blow with breath, or touch with hand,
Was like that music as it came; and then
Stream'd thro' my cell a cold and silver beam,
And down the long beam stole the Holy Grail,
Rose-red with beatings in it, as if alive,
Till all the white walls of my cell were dyed
With rosy colors leaping on the wall;

And then the music faded, and the Grail
Pass'd, and the beam decay'd, and from the walls
The rosy quiverings died into the night.
So now the Holy Thing is here again
Among us, brother, fast thou too and pray,
And tell thy brother knights to fast and pray,
That so perchance the vision may be seen
By thee and those, and all the world be heal'd.'

"Then leaving the pale nun, I spake of this
To all men; and myself fasted and pray'd
Always, and many among us many a week
Fasted and pray'd even to the uttermost,
Expectant of the wonder that would be.

"And one there was among us, ever moved
Among us in white armor, Galahad.
'God make thee good as thou art beautiful,'
Said Arthur, when he dubb'd him knight; and none,
In so young youth, was ever made a knight
Till Galahad; and this Galahad, when he heard
My sister's vision, fill'd me with amaze;
His eyes became so like her own, they seem'd
Hers, and himself her brother more than I.

"Sister or brother none had he; but some
Call'd him a son of Lancelot, and some said
Begotten by enchantment — chatterers they,
Like birds of passage piping up and down,
That gape for flies — we know not whence they come,
For when was Lancelot wanderingly lewd?

" But she, the wan sweet maiden shore away
Clean from her forehead all that wealth of hair
Which made a silken mat-work for her feet:
And out of this she plaited broad and long
A strong sword-belt, and wove with silver thread
And crimson in the belt a strange device,
A crimson grail within a silver beam;
And saw the bright boy-knight, and bound it on him,
Saying, ' My knight, my love, my knight of heaven,
O thou, my love, whose love is one with mine,
I, maiden, round thee, maiden, bind my belt.
Go forth, for thou shalt see what I have seen,
And break thro' all, till one will crown thee king
Far in the spiritual city:' and as she spake
She sent the deathless passion in her eyes
Thro' him, and made him hers, and laid her mind
On him, and he believed in her belief.

" Then came a year of miracle: O brother,
In our great hall there stood a vacant chair,
Fashion'd by Merlin ere he passed away,
And carven with strange figures; and in and on
The figures, like a serpent, ran a scroll
Of letters in a tongue no man could read.
And Merlin call'd it 'The Siege perilous,'
Perilous for good and ill; 'for there,' he said,
'No man could sit but he should lose himself:'
And once by misadventure Merlin sat
In his own chair, and so was lost; but he,
Galahad, when he heard of Merlin's doom,
Cried, 'If I lose myself I save myself!'

" Then on a summer night it came to pass,
While the great banquet lay along the hall,
That Galahad would sit down in Merlin's chair.

" And all at once, as there we sat, we heard
A cracking and a riving of the roofs,
And rending, and a blast, and overhead
Thunder, and in the thunder was a cry.

And in the blast there smote along the hall
A beam of light seven times more clear than day:
And down the long beam stole the Holy Grail
All over cover'd with a luminous cloud,
And none might see who bare it, and it past.
But every knight beheld his fellow's face
As in a glory, and all the knights arose,
And staring each at other like dumb men
Stood, till I found a voice and sware a vow

"I sware a vow before them all, that I
Because I had not seen the Grail, would ride
A twelvemonth and a day in quest of it,
Until I found and saw it, as the nun
My sister saw it; and Galahad sware the vow
And good Sir Bors, our Lancelot's cousin, sw
And Lancelot sware, and many among the kn
And Gawain sware, and louder than the rest.'

Then spake the monk Ambrosius, asking h
"What said the king? Did Arthur take the

"Nay, for my lord," said Percivale, "the Ki
Was not in hall: for early that same day,
'Scaped thro' a cavern from a bandit hold,
An outraged maiden sprang into the hall
Crying on help: for all her shining hair
Was smear'd with earth, and either milky arm
Red-rent with hooks of bramble, and all she v
Torn as a sail that leaves the rope is torn
In tempest:

"So the King arose and went
To smoke the scandalous hive of those wild bees
That made such honey in his realm. Howbeit
Some little of this marvel he too saw,
Returning o'er the plain that then began
To darken under Camelot; whence the King
Look'd up, calling aloud, ' Lo there ! the roofs
Of our great Hall are rolled in thunder-smoke !
Pray Heaven, they be not smitten by the bolt.'
For dear to Arthur was that hall of ours,
As having there so oft with all his knights
Feasted, and as the stateliest under heaven.

"O brother, had you known our mighty hall,
Which Merlin built for Arthur long ago!
For all the sacred mount of Camelot,
And all the dim rich city, roof by roof,
Tower after tower, spire beyond spire,
By grove, and garden-lawn, and rushing brook,
Climbs to the mighty hall that Merlin built.
And four great zones of sculpture, set betwixt
With many a mystic symbol, gird the hall:
And in the lowest beasts are slaying men,
And in the second men are slaying beasts,
And on the third are warriors, perfect men,
And on the fourth are men with growing wings,
And over all one statue in the mould
Of Arthur, made by Merlin, with a crown
And peak'd wings pointed to the Northern Star,
And eastward fronts the statue, and the crown
And both the wings are made of gold, and flame
At sunrise till the people in far fields,
Wasted so often by the heathen hordes,
Behold it, crying, 'We have still a king.'

"And, brother, had you known our hall within,
Broader and higher than any in all the lands!
Where twelve great windows blazon Arthur's wars,
And all the light that falls upon the board
Streams thro' the twelve great battles of our King.
Nay, one there is, and at the eastern end,
Wealthy with wandering lines of mount and mere,
Where Arthur finds the brand, Excalibur.
And also one to the west, and counter to it,
And blank: and who shall blazon it? when and how?—
O there, perchance, when all our wars are done,
The brand Excalibur will be cast away.

"So to this hall full quickly rode the King,
In horror lest the work by Merlin wrought,
Dreamlike, should on the sudden vanish, wrapt
In unremorseful folds of rolling fire.
And in he rode, and up I glanced, and saw
The golden dragon sparkling over all:

And many of those who burnt the hold, their arms
Hack'd, and their foreheads grimed with smoke, and scar'd
Follow'd, and in among bright faces, ours,
Full of the vision, prest: and then the King
Spake to me, being nearest, 'Percivale,'
(Because the hall was all in tumult — some
Vowing, and some protesting.) 'what is this?'

"O brother, when I told him what had chanced,
My sister's vision and the rest, his face
Darken'd, as I have seen it more than once,
When some brave deed seem'd to be done in vain,
Darken; and 'Woe is me, my knights!' he cried.
'Had I been here, ye had not sworn the vow.'
Bold was my answer, 'Had thyself been here,
My King, thou wouldst have sworn.' 'Yea, yea,' said he.
'Art thou so bold and hast not seen the Grail?'

"'Nay, Lord, I heard the sound, I saw the light,
But since I did not see the Holy Thing,
I sware a vow to follow it till I saw.'

"Then when he asked us, knight by knight, if any
Had seen it, all their answers were as one:
'Nay, Lord, and therefore have we sworn our vows.'

"'Lo now,' said Arthur, 'have ye seen a cloud?
What go ye into the wilderness to see?'

"Then Galahad on a sudden, and in a voice
Shrilling along the hall to Arthur, call'd,
'But I, Sir Arthur, saw the Holy Grail,
I saw the Holy Grail and heard a cry —
O Galahad, and O Galahad, follow me.'

But I, Sir Arthur, saw the Holy Grail

"'Ah, Galahad, Galahad,' said the King, 'for
As thou art is the vision, not for these.
Thy holy nun and thou have seen a sign —
Holier is none, my Percivale, than she —
A sign to maim this Order which I made.
But you, that follow but the leader's bell,'
(Brother, the king was hard upon his knights,)
'Taliessin is our fullest throat of song,
And one hath sung and all the dumb will sin;
Lancelot is Lancelot, and hath overborne
Five knights at once, and every younger knigh
Unproven, holds himself as Lancelot,
Till overborne by one, he learns — and ye,
What are ye? Galahads? — no, nor Percivale
(For thus it pleased the King to range me clo
After Sir Galahad); 'nay,' said he, 'but men
With strength and will to right the wrong'd, o
To lay the sudden heads of violence flat,
Knights that in twelve great battles splash'd a
The strong White Horse in his own heathen l

But one hath seen, and all the blind will see.
Go, since your vows are sacred, being made:
Yet — for ye know that the cries of all my realm,
Pass thro' this hall — how often, O my knights,
Your places being vacant at my side,
This chance of noble deeds will come and go
Unchallenged, while you follow wandering fires
Lost in the quagmire? many of you, yea most,
Return no more: ye think I show myself
Too dark a prophet: come now, let us meet
The morrow morn once more in one full field
Of gracious pastime, that once more the king,
Before you leave him for this Quest, may count
The yet-unbroken strength of all his knights,
Rejoicing in that Order which he made.'

  "So when the sun broke next from underground,
All the great table of our Arthur closed
And clash'd in such a tourney and so full,
So many lances broken — never yet
Had Camelot seen the like, since Arthur came:

And I myself and Galahad, for a strength
Was in us from the vision, overthrew
So many knights that all the people cried,
And almost burst the barriers in their heat,
Shouting 'Sir Galahad and Sir Percivale!'

　"But when the next day break from underground —
O brother, had you known our Camelot,
Built by old kings, age after age, so old
The king himself had fears that it would fall,
So strange, and rich, and dim; for where the roofs
Totter'd toward each other in the sky,
Met foreheads all along the street of those
Who watch'd us pass; and lower, and where the long
Rich galleries, lady-laden, weigh'd the necks
Of dragons clinging to the crazy walls,
Thicker than drops from thunder, showers of flowers
Fell as we past; and men and boys astride
On wyvern, lion, dragon, griffin, swan,
At all the corners, named us each by name,
Calling 'God speed!' but in the street below
The knights and ladies wept, and rich and poor
Wept,

"And the King himself could hardly speak
For grief, and in the middle street the Queen,
Who rode by Lancelot, wail'd and shriek'd aloud,
'This madness has come on us for our sins.'
And then we reach'd the wierdly sculptured gate,
Where Arthur's wars were render'd mystically,
And thence departed every one his way.

"And I was lifted up in heart, and thought
Of all my late-shown prowess in the lists,
How my strong lance had beaten down the knights,
So many and famous names; and never yet
Had heaven appear'd so blue, nor earth so green,
For all my blood danced in me, and I knew
That I should light upon the Holy Grail.

"Thereafter, the dark warning of our King,
That most of us would follow wandering fires,
Came like a driving gloom across my mind.
Then every evil word I had spoken once,
And every evil thought I had thought of old,
And every evil deed I ever did,
Awoke and cried, 'This Quest is not for thee.'

And lifting up mine eyes, I found myself
Alone, and in a land of sand and thorns,
And I was thirsty, even unto death;
And I, too, cried, 'This Quest is not for thee.'

    " And on I rode, and when I thought my thirst
Would slay me, saw deep lawns, and then a brook,
With one sharp rapid, where the crisping white
Play'd ever back upon the sloping wave,
And took both ear and eye; and o'er the brook
Were apple-trees, and apples by the brook
Fallen, and on the lawns, 'I will rest here,'
I said, 'I am not worthy of the Quest;'
But even while I drank the brook, and ate
The goodly apples, all these things at once
Fell into dust, and I was left alone,
And thirsting, in a land of sand and thorns.

    " And then behold a woman at a door
Spinning; and fair the house whereby she sat,
And kind the woman's eyes and innocent,
And all her bearing gracious; and she rose
Opening her arms to meet me, as who should say,
' Rest here;' but when I touched her, lo! she, too,

Fell into dust and nothing, and the house
Became no better than a broken shed,
And in it a dead babe; and also this
Fell into dust, and I was left alone.

   "And on I rode, and greater was my thirst.
Then flash'd a yellow gleam across the world,
And where it smote the ploughshare in the field,
The ploughman left his ploughing, and fell down
Before it; where it glitter'd on her pail,
The milkmaid left her milking, and fell down
Before it, and I knew not why, but thought
'The sun is rising,' tho' the sun had risen.
Then was I ware of one that on me moved
In golden armor with a crown of gold
About a casque all jewels; and his horse
In golden armor jewell'd everywhere:
And on the splendor came, flashing me blind;
And seem'd to me the Lord of all the world,
Being so huge. But when I thought he meant
To crush me, moving on me, lo! he, too,
Opened his arms to embrace me as he came.
And up I went and touch'd him, and he, too,
Fell into dust, and I was left alone
And wearying in a land of sand and thorns,

"And I rode on and found a mighty hill,
And on the top, a city wall'd; the spires
Prick'd with incredible pinnacles into heaven.
And by the gateway stirr'd a crowd; and these
Cried to me climbing, 'Welcome, Percivale!
Thou mightiest and thou purest among men!'
And glad was I and clomb, but found at top
No man, nor any voice. And thence I past
Far thro' a ruinous city, and I saw
That man had once dwelt there; but there I found
Only one man of an exceeding age.
'Where is that goodly company,' said I,
'That so cried out upon me?' and he had
Scarce any voice to answer, and yet gasp'd
'Whence and what art thou?' and even as he spoke
Fell into dust, and disappear'd, and I
Was left alone once more, and cried in grief,
'Lo, if I find the Holy Grail itself
And touch it, it will crumble into dust.'

"And thence I dropt into a lowly vale,
Low as the hill was high, and where the vale
Was lowest, found a chapel and thereby
A holy hermit in a hermitage,

To whom I told my phantoms, and he said:

" 'O son, thou hast not true humility,
The highest virtue, mother of them all;
For when the Lord of all things made Himself
Naked of glory for His mortal change,
"Take thou my robe," she said, "for all is thine."
And all her form shone forth with sudden light
So that the angels were amazed, and she
Follow'd him down, and like a flying star
Led on the gray-hair'd wisdom of the east;
But her thou hast not known: for what is this
Thou thoughtest of thy prowess and thy sins?
Thou hast not lost thyself to save thyself
As Galahad.' When the hermit made an end,
In silver armor suddenly Galahad shone
Before us, and against the chapel door
Laid lance, and enter'd, and we knelt in prayer.
And there the hermit slaked my burning thirst,
And at the sacring of the mass I saw
The holy elements alone; but he:
'Saw ye no more? I, Galahad, saw the Grail,
The Holy Grail, descend upon the shrine:
I saw the fiery face as of a child

That smote itself into the bread, and went;
And hither am I come; and never yet
Hath what thy sister taught me first to see,
This Holy Thing, fail'd from my side, nor come
Cover'd, but moving with me night and day,
Fainter by day, but always in the night
Blood-red, and sliding down the blacken'd mars!
Blood-red, and on the naked mountain top
Blood-red, and in the sleeping mere below
Blood-red. And in the strength of this I rode,
Shattering all evil customs everywhere,
And past thro' Pagan realms, and made them
And clash'd with Pagan hordes, and bore them
And broke thro' all, and in the strength of this
Come victor. But my time is hard at hand.
And hence I go; and one will crown me king
Far in the spiritual city; and come thou, too,
For thou shalt see the vision when I go.'

"While thus he spake, his eye, dwelling on
Drew me, with power upon me, till I grew
One with him, to believe as he believed.
Then, when the day began to wane, we went.

"There rose a hill that none but man could climb,
Scarr'd with a hundred wintry watercourses —
Storm at the top, and when we gain'd it, storm
Round us and death; for every moment glanced
His silver arms and gloom'd: so quick and thick
The lightnings here and there to left and right
Struck, till the dry old trunks about us, dead,
Yea, rotten with a hundred years of death,
Sprang into fire: and at the base we found
On either hand, as far as eye could see,
A great black swamp and of an evil smell,
Part black, part whiten'd with the bones of men,
Not to be crost, save that some ancient king
Had built a way, where, link'd with many a bridge,
A thousand piers ran into the great Sea.
And Galahad fled along them bridge by bridge,
And every bridge as quickly as he crost
Sprang into fire and vanish'd, tho' I yearn'd
To follow, and thrice above him all the heavens
Open'd and blazed with thunder such as seem'd
Shoutings of all the sons of God:

And first

At once I saw him far on the great Sea.
In silver-shining armor starry-clear;
And o'er his head the holy vessel hung
Clothed in white samite or a luminous cloud.
And with exceeding swiftness ran the boat
If boat it were — I saw not whence it came.
And when the heavens open'd and blazed again
Roaring, I saw him like a silver star —
And had he set the sail, or had the boat
Become a living creature clad with wings?
And o'er his head the holy vessel hung
Redder than any rose, a joy to me,
For now I knew the veil had been withdrawn.
Then in a moment when they blazed again
Opening, I saw the least of little stars
Down on the waste, and straight beyond the star
I saw the spiritual city and all her spires
And gateways in a glory like one pearl —
No larger, tho' the goal of all the saints —
Strike from the sea; and from the star there shot
A rose-red sparkle to the city, and there
Dwelt, and I knew it was the Holy Grail,
Which never eyes on earth again shall see.

Then fell the floods of heaven drowning the deep,
And how my feet recross'd the deathful ridge
No memory in me lives; but that I touch'd
The chapel-doors at dawn I know; and thence
Taking my war-horse from the holy man,
Glad that no phantom vext me more, return'd
To whence I came, the gate of Arthur's wars."

  " O brother," ask'd Ambrosius, — " for in sooth
These ancient books — and they would win thee — teem,
Only I find not there this Holy Grail,
With miracles and marvels like to these,
Not all unlike; which oftentime I read,
Who read but on my breviary with ease,
Till my head swims; and then go forth and pass
Down to the little thorpe that lies so close,
And almost plaster'd like a martin's nest
To these old walls — and mingle with our folk;
And knowing every honest face of theirs,
As well as ever shepherd knew his sheep,
And every homely secret in their hearts,
Delight myself with gossip and old wives,
And ills and aches, and teethings, lyings-in,

And mirthful sayings, children of the place
That have no meaning half a league away:
Or lulling random squabbles when they rise,
Chafferings and chatterings at the market-cross,
Rejoice, small man, in this small world of mine,
Yea, even in their hens and in their eggs, —
O brother, saving this Sir Galahad
Came ye on none but phantoms in your quest,
No man, no woman?"

                        Then, Sir Percivale:
"All men, to one so bound by such a vow,
And women were as phantoms. O my brother,
Why wilt thou shame me to confess to thee
How far I falter'd from my quest and vow?
For after I had lain so many nights
A bedmate of the snail and eft and snake,
In grass and burdock, I was changed to wan
And meagre, and the vision had not come.
And then I chanced upon a goodly town
With one great dwelling in the middle of it;
Thither I made, and there was I disarm'd
By maidens each as fair as any flower:

But when they led me into hall, behold
The Princess of that castle was the one,
Brother, and that one only, who had ever
Made my heart leap; for when I moved of old
A slender page about her father's hall,
And she a slender maiden, all my heart
Went after her with longing: yet we twain
Had never kiss'd a kiss, or vow'd a vow.
And now I came upon her once again,
And one had wedded her, and he was dead,
And all his land and wealth and state were hers.
And while I tarried, every day she set
A banquet richer than the day before
By me; for all her longing and her will
Was toward me as of old: till one fair morn,
I walking to and fro beside a stream
That flash'd across her orchard underneath
Her castle-walls, she stole upon my walk,
And calling me the greatest of all knights,
Embraced me, and so kiss'd me the first time,
And gave herself and all her wealth to me.

Then I remember'd Arthur's warning word,
That most of us would follow wandering fires,
And the Quest faded in my heart. Anon,
The heads of all her people drew to me,
With supplication both of knees and tongue.
'We have heard of thee: thou art our greatest knight;
Our Lady says it, and we well believe:
Wed thou our Lady, and rule over us,
And thou shalt be as Arthur in our land.'
O me, my brother! but one night my vow
Burnt me within, so that I rose and fled,
But wail'd and wept, and hated mine own self,
And ev'n the Holy Quest, and all but her;
Then after I was join'd with Galahad
Cared not for her, nor anything upon earth."

Then said the monk, " Poor men, when yule is cold,
Must be content to sit by little fires.

And this am I, so that ye care for me
Ever so little; yea, and blest be Heaven
That brought thee here to this poor house of ours,
Where all the brethren are so hard, to warm
My cold heart with a friend; but O the pity
To find thine own first love once more — to hold,
Hold her a wealthy bride within thine arms,
Or all but hold, and then — cast her aside,
Foregoing all her sweetness, like a weed.
For we that want the warmth of double life,
We that are plagued with dreams of something sweet
Beyond all sweetness in a life so rich, —
Ah, blessed Lord, I speak too earthlywise,
Seeing I never stray'd beyond the cell,
But live like an old badger in his earth,
With earth about him everywhere, despite
All fast and penance. Saw ye none beside,
None of your knights?"

             " Yea so," said Percivale :

" One night my pathway swerving east, I saw
The pelican on the casque of our Sir Bors
All in the middle of the rising moon:

And toward him spurr'd and hail'd him, and he me,
And each made joy of either; then he ask'd.
'Where is he? hast thou seen him — Lancelot? Once,'
Said good Sir Bors, 'he dash'd across me — mad,
And maddening what he rode: and when I cried,
" Ridest thou then so hotly on a quest
So holy?" Lancelot shouted, " Stay me not!
I have been the sluggard, and I ride apace,
For now there is a lion in the way."
So vanish'd.'

                    " Then Sir Bors had ridden on
Softly, and sorrowing for our Lancelot,
Because his former madness, once the talk
And scandal of our table, had return'd:
For Lancelot's kith and kin so worship him
That ill to him is ill to them; to Bors
Beyond the rest: he well had been content
Not to have seen, so Lancelot might have seen,
The Holy Cup of healing; and, indeed,

Being so clouded with his grief and love,
Small heart was his after the Holy Quest:
If God would send the vision, well: if not,
The Quest and he were in the hands of Heaven.

   " And then, with small adventure met, Sir Bors
Rode to the lonest tract of all the realm,
And found a people there among their crags,
Our race and blood, a remnant that were left
Paynim amid their circles, and the stones
They pitch up straight to heaven: and their wise men
Were strong in that old magic which can trace
The wandering of the stars, and scoff'd at him,
And this High Quest as at a simple thing:
Told him he follow'd — almost Arthur's words
A mocking fire: ' what other fire than he,
Whereby the blood beats, and the blossom blows,
And the sea rolls, and all the world is warm'd ? '
And when his answer chafed them, the rough crowd,
Hearing he had a difference with their priests,
Seized him, and bound and plunged him into a cell
Of great piled stones :

                          " And lying bounden there
In darkness thro' innumerable hours
He heard the hollow-ringing heavens sweep
Over him, till by miracle — what else?
Heavy as it was, a great stone slipt and fell,
Such as no wind could move : and thro' the gap
Glimmer'd the streaming scud : then came a night
Still as the day was loud ; and thro' the gap
The seven clear stars of Arthur's Table Round —
For, brother, so one night, because they roll
Thro' such a round in heaven, we named the stars,
Rejoicing in ourselves and in our king —
And these, like bright eyes of familiar friends,
In on him shone, ' And then to me, to me,'
Said good Sir Bors, ' beyond all hopes of mine,
Who scarce had pray'd or ask'd it for myself —
Across the seven clear stars — O grace to me —
In color like the fingers of a hand
Before a burning taper, the sweet Grail
Glided and past, and close upon it peal'd
A sharp quick thunder.'

                 " Afterwards a maid,
Who kept our holy faith among her kin
In secret, entering loosed and let him go."

    To whom the monk: " And I remember now
That pelican on the casque: Sir Bors it was
Who spake so low and sadly at our board;
And mighty reverent at our grace was he:
A square-set man and honest; and his eyes,
An out-door sign of all the warmth within,
Smiled with his lips — a smile beneath a cloud,
But Heaven had meant it for a sunny one:
Ay, ay, Sir Bors, who else? But when ye reach'd
The city, found ye all your knights return'd,
Or was there sooth in Arthur's prophecy,
Tell me, and what said each, and what the King ?

    Then answer'd Percivale: " And that can I,
Brother, and truly; since the living words
Of so great men as Lancelot and our King
Pass not from door to door and out again,
But sit within the house.

                              " O, when we reach'd
The city, our horses stumbling as they trode
On heaps of ruin,

"Hornless unicorns.
Crack'd basilisks, and splinter'd cockatrices,
And shatter'd talbots, which had left the stones
Raw, that they fell from, brought us to the hall.

"And there sat Arthur on the daïs-throne,
And those that had gone out upon the Quest,
Wasted and worn, and but a tithe of them,
And those that had not, stood before the King,
Who, when he saw me, rose, and bade me hail,
Saying, 'A welfare in thine eye reproves
Our fear of some disastrous chance for thee
On hill, or plain, at sea, or flooding ford.
So fierce a gale made havoc here of late
Among the strange devices of our kings;
Yea, shook this newer, stronger hall of ours,
And from the statue Merlin moulded for us
Half wrench'd a golden wing; but now — the quest
This vision — hast thou seen the Holy Cup,
That Joseph brought of old to Glastonbury?'

"So when I told him all thyself hast heard,

Ambrosius, and my fresh but fixt resolve
To pass away into the quiet life,
He answer'd not, but, sharply turning, ask'd
Of Gawain, 'Gawain, was this Quest for thee?'

   "'Nay, lord,' said Gawain, 'not for such as I
Therefore I communed with a saintly man,
Who made me sure the Quest was not for me.
For I was much awearied of the Quest;
But found a silk pavilion in a field,
And merry maidens in it; and then this gale
Tore my pavilion from the tenting-pin,
And blew my merry maidens all about
With all discomfort; yea, and but for this,
My twelvemonth and a day were pleasant to me.'

   "He ceased; and Arthur turn'd to whom at first
He saw not, for Sir Bors, on entering, push'd
Athwart the throng to Lancelot, caught his hand,
Held it, and there, half hidden by him, stood,

Until the King espied him, saying to him,
'Hail, Bors! if ever loyal man and true
Could see it, thou hast seen the Grail;' and Bors,
'Ask me not, for I may not speak of it.
I saw it:' and the tears were in his eyes —

"Then there remain'd but Lancelot, for the rest
Spake but of sundry perils in the storm:
Perhaps, like him of Cana in Holy Writ,
Our Arthur kept his best until the last.
'Thou, too, my Lancelot,' ask'd the King, 'my friend,
Our mightiest, hath this Quest avail'd for thee?'"

"'Our mightiest!' answer'd Lancelot, with a groan;
'O King!'—and when he paused, methought I spied
A dying fire of madness in his eyes,—
'O King, my friend, if friend of thine I be,
Happier are those that welter in their sin,
Swine in the mud, that cannot see for slime,

Slime of the ditch: but in me lived a sin
So strange, of such a kind, that all of pure,
Noble, and knightly in me twined and clung
Round that one sin, until the wholesome flower
And poisonous grew together, each as each,
Not to be pluck'd asunder; and when thy knights
Sware, I sware with them only in the hope
That could I touch or see the Holy Grail
They might be pluck'd asunder: then I spake
To one most holy saint, who wept and said,
That save they could be pluck'd asunder, all
My quest were but in vain; to whom I vow'd
That I would work according as he will'd.
And forth I went, and while I yearn'd and strove
To tear the twain asunder in my heart,
My madness came upon me as of old,
And whipt me into waste fields far away;
There was I beaten down by little men,

Mean knights, to whom the moving of my sword
And shadow of my spear had been enow
To scare them from me once; and then I came
All in my folly to the naked shore,
Wide flats, where nothing but coarse grasses grew
But such a blast, my King, began to blow,
So loud a blast along the shore and sea,
Ye could not hear the waters for the blast,
Tho' heapt in mounds and ridges all the sea
Drove like a cataract, and all the sand
Swept like a river, and the clouded heavens
Were shaken with the motion and the sound.
And blackening in the sea-foam sway'd a boat,
Half swallow'd in it, anchor'd with a chain;
And in my madness to myself I said,
" I will embark and I will lose myself,
And in the great sea wash away my sin."
I burst the chain, I sprang into the boat.

Seven days I drove along the dreary deep,

And with me drove the moon and all the stars;
And the wind fell, and on the seventh night
I heard the shingle grinding in the surge,
And felt the boat shock earth, and looking up,
Behold, the enchanted towers of Carbonek,
A castle like a rock upon a rock,
With chasm-like portals open to the sea,
And steps that met the breaker! there was none
Stood near it but a lion on each side
That kept the entry, and the moon was full.
Then from the boat I leapt, and up the stairs.
There drew my sword. With sudden-flaring manes
Those two great beasts rose upright like a man,
Each gript a shoulder, and I stood between:
And, when I would have smitten them, heard a vo
" Doubt not, go forward; if thou doubt, the beasts
Will tear thee piecemeal;"

"Then with violence
The sword was dash'd from out my hand, and fell.
And up into the sounding hall I past;
But nothing in the sounding hall I saw,
No bench nor table, painting on the wall
Or shield of knight; only the rounded moon
Thro' the tall oriel on the rolling sea.
But always in the quiet house I heard,
Clear as a lark, high o'er me as a lark,
A sweet voice singing in the topmost tower
To the eastward: up I climb'd a thousand steps
With pain: as in a dream I seem'd to climb
Forever: at the last I reach'd a door,
A light was in the crannies, and I heard,
"Glory and joy and honor to our Lord
And to the Holy Vessel of the Grail."
Then in my madness I essay'd the door;

It gave, and thro' a stormy glare, a heat
As from a seventimes-heated furnace, I,
Blasted and burnt, and blinded as I was,
With such a fierceness that I swoon'd away —
O, yet methought I saw the Holy Grail,
All pall'd in crimson samite, and around
Great angels, awful shapes, and wings and eyes,
And but for all my madness and my sin,
And then my swooning, I had sworn I saw
That which I saw; but what I saw was veil'd
And cover'd; and this quest was not for me.'

    " So speaking, and here ceasing, Lancelot left
The hall long silent, till Sir Gawain — nay,
Brother, I need not tell thee foolish words, —
A reckless and irreverent knight was he,
Now bolden'd by the silence of his King,

Well, I will tell thee : 'O King, my liege,' he said,
'Hath Gawain fail'd in any quest of thine?
When have I stinted stroke in foughten field?
But as for thine, my good friend, Percivale,
Thy holy nun and thou have driven men mad,
Yea, made our mightiest madder than our least.
But by mine eyes and by mine ears I swear,
I will be deafer than the blue-eyed cat,
And thrice as blind as any noonday owl,
To holy virgins in their ecstasies,
Henceforward."

   "'Deafer,' said the blameless King,
'Gawain, and blinder unto holy things
Hope not to make thyself by idle vows,
Being too blind to have desire to see.
But if indeed there came a sign from heaven,

Blessed are Bors, Lancelot, and Percivale,
For these have seen according to their sight.
For every fiery prophet in old times,
And all the sacred madness of the bard,
When God made music thro' them, could but speak
His music by the framework and the chord;
And as ye saw it ye have spoken truth.

"'Nay — but thou errest, Lancelot: never
Could all of true and noble in knight and man
Twine round one sin, whatever it may be,
With such a closeness, but apart there grew,
Save that he were the swine thou spakest of,
Some root of knighthood and pure nobleness;
Whereto see thou, that it may bear its flower.

"'And spake I not too truly, O my knights?
Was I too dark a prophet when I said
To those who went upon the Holy Quest,
That most of them would follow wandering fires,

Lost in the quagmire? — lost to me and

And left me gazing at a barren board,

And a lean Order — scarce return'd a t

And out of those to whom the vision c

My greatest hardly will believe he saw;

Another hath beheld it afar off,

And leaving human wrongs to right the

Cares but to pass into the silent life.

And one hath had the vision face to fa

And now his chair desires him here in

However they may crown him otherwhe

"'And some among you held, that if

Had seen the sight he would have swor

Not easily, seeing that the King must g

That which he rules, and is but as the

To whom a space of land is given to p

Who may not wander from the alotted field,
Before his work be done; but, being done,
Let visions of the night or of the day
Come, as they will: and many a time they come,
Until this earth he walks on seems not earth,
This light that strikes his eyeball is not light,
This air that smites his forehead is not air
But vision — yea, his very hands and feet —
In moments when he feels he cannot die,
And knows himself no vision to himself,
Nor the high God a vision, nor that One
Who rose again: ye have seen what ye have seen.'

www.ingramcontent.com/pod-product-compliance
Lightning Source LLC
Chambersburg PA
CBHW032358020726
47499CB00008B/2806